Cookham Library
High Road
Cookham Rise
SL6 9JF
el: 01628 5261
KT-148-112

Molly Mischief

Saves the World!

Windsor and Maidenhead
95800000077403

First published in the United Kingdom in 2018 by
Pavilion Children's Books
43 Great Ormond Street
London
WC1N 3HZ

An imprint of Pavilion Books Limited

Publisher and Editor: Neil Dunnicliffe
Art Director and Designer: Lee-May Lim

All rights reserved. No part of this publication may be reproduced, stored in a retrieval system, or transmitted in any form or by any means electronic, mechanical, photocopying, recording or otherwise, without prior permission of the copyright owner

Text and illustrations © Adam Hargreaves 2018

The moral rights of the author and illustrator have been asserted

ISBN: 9781843653585

A CIP catalogue record for this book is available from the British Library

10 9 8 7 6 5 4 3 2 1

Reproduction by Mission, Hong Kong
Printed by Toppan Leefung Printing Ltd, China

This book can be ordered directly from the publisher online
at www.pavilionbooks.com, or try your local bookshop.

Molly Mischief

Saves the World!

Adam Hargreaves

PAVILION

Hello, my name is **Molly.**
Most of the time I'm happy – happy making mischief.

That's why I'm called **Molly Mischief!**

But some things make me unhappy. Things like chores.

I don't like tidying my room.
But when I *do* tidy my room, Mum's not happy!

There's no pleasing her.

I don't like unpacking the groceries.
But when I *do* unpack the groceries, Dad's not happy.
There's no pleasing him!
Food
Food
Fruit Gloops
MOLLY!

And I don't like washing up.
But when I *do* the washing up, my brother's not happy.

Sometimes there's no pleasing anyone!

MOLLY!

I wish I could do all my chores in supersonic time.
I wish I had superpowers.
I wish I could be a superhero.

So I went upstairs and got dressed as...

SUPER-MOLLY!

I tidied my bedroom in super-quick time.

I vacuumed,
SUPER-MOLLY!
and polished,
SUPER-MOLLY!

put away the dishes,

SUPER-MOLLY!

mopped, SUPER-MOLLY!

and took out the rubbish. ALL in the blink of an eye!

M
I had *lots* of superpowers.
I was very **STRONG.**
I had **LASER EYES.**
N

I could walk on the ceiling.
Woof!
Woof!
Woof!
Woof!
Woof!
I could talk to animals.
I could leap over
TALL
buildings in
a single bound!

And I could fly!

Up! Up! Up!

And away!

I discovered I could drink
15 milkshakes in 15 seconds!

Although I am not sure that
was such a good idea.

I could fly my kite,
even when there was no wind!
19
And you ought to have seen me on my bike!

It was great fun having lots of superpowers.

It was also very useful.
It was useful when the bully at school tried to take my lunch money.

And it was useful when we
got stuck in a traffic jam.

I helped an old lady cross the road, at ***super speed.***

And then I realised I could be a real-life superhero.

I saved a cow from a tornado.
MOO!

I rescued a **whale** at the seaside!

Sport
Super-Molly wins the Tour de Bike
Daily News
Super-Molly Saves Cow!

And I saved the world
from a meteorite!

Super-Molly became super-famous.
She was on the front page of the paper and starred on the TV news.

But nobody knew it was me.
Nobody knew all the good deeds I was doing.
It's no fun being famous and not being recognised.
It's no fun being good and not getting praise.

Being a superhero was also hard work.
I had to get up in the middle of the night to fight crime.

M
I had to miss my favourite dinner to capture an escaped lion.

And cleaning up the flood was no fun at all.

In fact, being a superhero was just one long list of chores!

So, I gave up being Super-Molly.

I decided it was much easier to do what I'm told.
Well, most of the time.

I *have* kept one superpower.
One superpower I would never give up.
I am super...

...Mischievous!